for nana and her
magical stories

-Michele

for all those looking for a smile
to fall upon their faces

-Jazmin

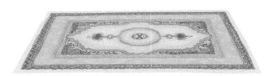

Illustrations and Book Design by Jazmin Welch

Balboa Press books may be ordered
through booksellers or by contacting:

Balboa Press
A Division of Hay House
1663 Liberty Drive
Bloomington, IN 47403
www.balboapress.com
1 (877) 407-4847

ISBN: 978-1-9822-0340-5 (sc)
ISBN: 978-1-9822-0341-2 (e)

Library of Congress Control Number: 2018906554

Print information available on the last page.

Balboa Press rev. date: 06/11/2018

BALBOA
PRESS
A DIVISION OF HAY HOUSE

sitting with auntie

BY MICHELE WELCH

ILLUSTRATED BY JAZMIN WELCH

"Auntie, WHAT are you doing?"

"Meditating."

"Can I try?"

"Sure."

Adam grabbed a cushion from the couch, tossed it on the floor beside his Aunt and plopped down.

He carefully crossed his legs
and rested his hands on his knees,
just like Auntie was doing.

"What's next?" Adam asked,
wondering if this was IT?

"Well," Auntie slowly revealed,

"We listen for our beautiful *heartbeat*."

"Can you hear it?"

Adam thought, "Nope," and was about to jump back up when Auntie whispered…

"Feel your breath on the tip of your nose
and breathe it down into your belly.
Breathe in 1, 2, 3
and follow it back out, 1, 2, 3, 4.
Now let's do it again."

Then, Auntie placed Adam's hand over
his heart and said, "Listen with your hand."

As the two of them sat in silence their
breathing softened

and

calmed.

"I can hear it!" whispered Adam.
There it was, his heartbeat!
"Yes, isn't it magnificent?"

Adam smiled, jumped up, grabbed his hat and
declared that it was time to play.

Auntie's smile widened.

Later that day, Adam came storming
into the house.
He was **REALLY** angry.

He stomped his feet, pushed his
toys out of the way, and growled
and scowled at
everyone
in
his
path.

His **MAD** face was squished up tight. "I'm really mad," thought Adam.

And then he thought about the playground.

And he thought about his favorite hat.

And he thought about how they wouldn't **GIVE IT BACK**!

He felt **MAD,**

MAD,

MAD!

He threw himself down onto
a cushion on the floor.

All of a sudden, his body
remembered the stillness of his
meditation time with Auntie, and
s l o w l y,
his breathing
    settled
        down.

1, 2, 3 breathe in,
down to the belly, and
1, 2, 3, 4, breathe back out.

In and out.

There it was...

his magnificent *heartbeat*.

His anger melted.

His mad face, mad stomp, mad growl,
and mad thoughts drifted off.

Adam felt a lot better, so he headed
out to play.

THERE was his hat, right beside the
big curvy slide.

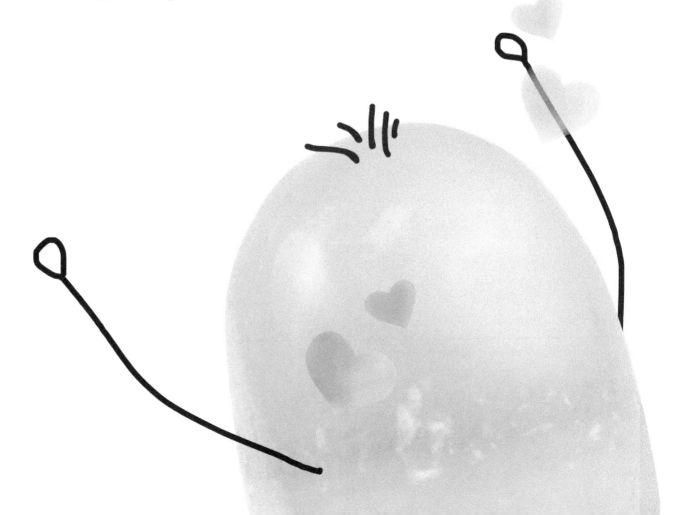

He scooped it up, put it on,
and felt his smile grow and grow,

just like Auntie's.

NOTE TO PARENTS AND TEACHERS

Why use a breathing meditation?

Using the breath is a wonderful way to proactively teach children to recognize their emotions, and also to calm down during stressful situations.

Deep and slow breathing gives the brain a chance to move from working in the emotional, fight or flight, **reactionary brain** (the amygdala), to the reasoning and **thinking brain** (the prefrontal cortex). In this way, life's stressful situations have a chance to be less dramatic and put more into perspective.

Breathing meditations are totally portable and can be practised anytime and anywhere: in waiting rooms, on car trips, during study and homework time or even at bedtime. I hope you enjoy this gentle step onto the meditation path and can share it with the children in your life.

Here are a few more breathing techniques to try:

Star Finger Breathing: Hold one hand up with the fingers spread open wide. Using the pointer finger of the other hand, imagine painting brilliant sparkles on each finger as it is slowly traced. Breathe in while tracing up, and breathe out while tracing down the other side of the finger. Switch hands, and repeat. Alternatively, children may like to trace a parent or another child's hand or even trace their own hand on paper while practising with the breath.

Going for a Ride Breathing: This technique can be done lying down with the child's hands or small toy on the belly. The hands or toy can go for a ride up and down the belly hill as the child slowly and deeply breathes in and out, allowing the belly to gently rise and fall. Repeat for 5-10 seconds.

Thank you for joining me.

Michele

MICHELE WELCH is a teacher, mother and auntie with degrees in Drama and Education. She began her quest to learn more about stress and mental health after studying meditation with Master Ilse Gordon, at The Centre of Awareness. Currently, she continues to learn, practise, teach, and write about simple, useful, meditation/ mindfulness tools to help both adults and children thrive. She lives in Toronto, with her husband and ever-growing gemstone rock collection. You can find two of her favourite gemstones as characters in *Sitting With Auntie*. Visit her at SmoothRockMeditation.com.

JAZMIN WELCH is an illustrator and book designer based in Toronto. After receiving art and design training, she started to play with abstract lines and contours and now prefers the playful aspects of a single line to realistic renderings. She works on a wide range of book designs from academic texts to novels, journals, and children's books. Jazmin is the founder and creative director of fleck creative. Visit fleckcreativestudio.com to learn more.

CPSIA information can be obtained
at www.ICGtesting.com
Printed in the USA
LVHW07s0536100818
586421LV00004B/5/P